STAR WARS®

EPISODE I

ADVENTURES

The Fury of Darth Maul

Ryder Windham

LUCAS BOOKS

SCHOLASTIC INC.

New York Toronto London Auckland Sydney
Mexico City New Delhi Hong Kong

ISBN 0-439-10140-9

12 11 10 9 8 7 6 5 4 3 2 1   9/9 0 1 2 3 4/0

Printed in the U.S.A.
First Scholastic printing, November 1999

INTRODUCTION

On the planet Esseles in the Darpa Sector, the Trade Federation had recently forced a Kloodavian manufacturer named Trinkatta to secretly build fifty droid starfighters. The Trade Federation provided Trinkatta with a prototype hyperdrive engine and had him duplicate the engine for installation into each starfighter. With hyperdrive capability, the droid starfighters could be deployed for long-range sneak attacks to almost any point in the galaxy.

Trinkatta's test pilot, Bama Vook, hoped to prevent the Trade Federation from obtaining such dangerous weapons. Bama sent a data card to alert the Jedi Council on Coruscant, telling them what was going on.

After Trinkatta's droids loaded the fighters onto a freighter, Bama Vook and his droid Leeper stole the entire freighter and hid it in a Calamar City docking bay on Esseles. Unfortunately, Bama and Leeper did not realize the freighter belonged to a hive of Bartokk assassins. The bloodthirsty Bartokks had conspired to steal the droid starfighters themselves, and reprogrammed Trinkatta's droids to take over his starship factory.

Jedi Master Adi Gallia was sent to investigate Trinkatta's factory, but she was captured by the reprogrammed droids before she could act. Jedi Master Qui-Gon Jinn, his Padawan Apprentice Obi-Wan Kenobi, and the Jedi Knights Vel Ardox and

Noro Zak went to rescue Master Adi from the renegade droids. They learned the droids had been reprogrammed by the Bartokks, and assumed the assassins intended to use the starfighters for a deadly assignment.

Because Master Adi was wounded, Vel and Noro took her to a Jedi chapter house on Rhinnal, a nearby planet that was famed throughout the Darpa Sector for its citizens' medical expertise. Meanwhile, Qui-Gon, Obi-Wan, and Trinkatta remained on Rhinnal to look for Bama Vook and the fifty droid starfighters. They found Bama and Leeper . . . and a band of vengeful Bartokk assassins.

The Bartokks kidnapped Bama's hulking young son Chup-Chup, then made a daring escape from Esseles in the freighter. Fortunately, the freighter was not capable of flying at lightspeed, and a lone hero was able to catch up with the fleeing ship. Chup-Chup was saved and the Neimoidian prototype hyperdrive engine was retrieved. Since the freighter had been on a programmed course for the planet Corulag, it was assumed this was the Bartokks' target.

The freighter and its cargo were destroyed to prevent it from reaching Corulag, but the danger was far from over. The Bartokks had transferred twenty-five starfighters to a second freighter.

Obi-Wan used a subspace transceiver to transmit a warning to Corulag. He also sent a message to Rhinnal, but no response came from the Jedi chapter house. Concerned for the safety of Adi Gallia and the other Jedi, Qui-Gon insisted on traveling to Rhinnal immediately.

As for the second Bartokk freighter, Qui-Gon was confident that he and Obi-Wan could still locate the sluggish vessel before it reached its destination.

At this time in history, the Jedi believed their mortal enemy, the Sith, had been extinct for over a thousand years. Thus, Qui-Gon and Obi-Wan did not have any idea that the Trade Federation's hyperdrive-equipped droid starfighters were part of a plan devised by an evil Sith Lord named Darth Sidious.

After Darth Sidious learned from Neimoidian spies that the droid starfighters had been stolen by the Bartokks, he decided the assassins would have to be punished.

He summoned his dark apprentice, Darth Maul.

CHAPTER ONE

Twilight fell over Galactic City. The mirrored surfaces of countless skyscrapers reflected the deep velvet sky, and every building was speckled by illuminated windows. Such spires covered the entire planet of Coruscant, ensuring that the sweeping views were enjoyed only by those who lived within the highest towers. The uppermost levels were reserved for prominent dignitaries, influential politicians, and the wealthiest citizens. Most of these people believed that Supreme Chancellor Valorum of the Galactic Senate was the most powerful person on all of Coruscant.

They were wrong.

Darth Sidious stood on his balcony, watching a thin, pink cloud drift slowly across the sky until it vanished behind a distant tower. Concealed by his black robes, the Sith Lord's face was lost in shadow. He watched as the cloud reappeared on the other side of the obscuring tower. Its color had changed to a deep bloodred.

Although Darth Sidious did not hear anyone enter his secret lair, he sensed a great malevolence flow into the room. From behind him, a deep voice spoke, "What is thy bidding, my Master?"

Darth Sidious remained on the balcony and kept his eyes on the crimson cloud. "The Neimoidian spies on Esseles have reported the fifty droid starfighters and prototype hyperdrive engine were seized by a Bartokk freighter. The Bartokks were probably hired to kill someone, and I imagine they intended to use the starfighters so the Trade Federation would appear responsible. As you know, those starfighters were crucial to our plan to take over the planet Brentaal and control the Perlemian Trade Route and the Hydian Way. Unfortunately, it seems the Jedi have learned about the droid starfighters. Since we cannot yet risk revealing ourselves to them, our effort to conquer Brentaal must be postponed."

"What about the starfighters?" the voice behind Darth Sidious asked.

"That's where you come in, my young apprentice," Darth Sidious answered, turning to face Darth Maul.

Like his Master, the second Sith Lord was also clad in black, but Darth Maul's face was covered in a broad, jagged black-and-red pattern. His cloak was pulled back to reveal the short, hooked horns that studded his hairless head. Within the dimly lit room, Maul's yellow eyes burned with evil.

"The starfighters were constructed at great expense, but they are worthless if the Jedi suspect that the Trade Federation intends to use them to attack Brentaal," Darth Sidious intoned as he handed a data card to Darth Maul. "Install this data card into your starship's computer. It will enable you to control the droid starfighters. Then go to the Esseles system and track the Bartokk freighter. Retrieve the starfighters if you can, and destroy them if you must. The Bartokks must be discouraged from any attempt to implicate the Trade Federation in their murderous schemes. If they were hired to steal the starfighters, their client must be identified and taught not to meddle with Trade Federation property."

"Do you want the Bartokks' clients to be eliminated?" Darth Maul inquired.

"No," Darth Sidious answered. "Let them live in terror. Their fear will spread, and we will use it to our advantage."

"And what of the Bartokks themselves?"

"Do with them as you please."

Darth Maul's lips twitched back to reveal sharp, black and yellow teeth. "Yes, my lord."

Bama Vook's bulky Corellian freighter, the *Metron Burner*, rose into the air from Trinkatta's barricaded starship factory. The Jedi's landspeeder and the captured Neimoidian prototype hyperdrive engine were both secured within the *Metron Burner*'s main hold. In the cockpit, Qui-Gon Jinn and Obi-Wan Kenobi were seated behind Bama and his droid copilot, Leeper.

Peering through the cockpit viewport, Leeper's photoreceptors gazed down to the spaceport's tarmac, where Bama's son Chup-Chup and Trinkatta the Kloodavian waved good-bye. "It looks like

Trinkatta's right arm has almost regenerated," the droid commented.

Bama cast a glance back to Qui-Gon. "You're sure Chup-Chup will be safe with Trinkatta?" the Talz bellowed over the *Metron Burner*'s roaring repulsorlift engines. "I can't help being afraid the Neimoidians or the Bartokks might return to Trinkatta's factory."

"I understand your concern," Qui-Gon replied. "Obi-Wan transmitted our report to the Jedi Council, informing them that the Bartokks stole what appeared to be Trade Federation droid starfighters. Since the Trade Federation is violating over a dozen intergalactic laws by constructing ships outside their own territory, they will probably deny they commissioned Trinkatta to build the starfighters. If they don't want trouble with the Republic, they'll stay away from Esseles for a long, long time. As for the Bartokks, it seems their mission is taking them to Corulag. I doubt they'll return to Esseles."

"That's not exactly reassuring," Bama grumbled as the *Metron Burner* broke away from Esseles atmosphere.

Before Qui-Gon Jinn could offer additional consolation, Leeper warned, "Hang on tight. We're almost at the hyperspace jump point."

Qui-Gon looked to Obi-Wan. Tension was visible in the young man's face. "I know what you're thinking, Padawan," Qui-Gon said in hushed voice. "You think we should be pursuing the Bartokk freighter."

Obi-Wan returned his Master's gaze. "Just because the first freighter was only outfitted with a sublight drive is no reason to assume the second freighter isn't faster. For all we know, it may have almost reached Corulag by now."

"Then we'll just have to make every effort to get to Corulag before the Bartokks," Qui-Gon calmly replied. "Rhinnal is our first priority."

"I don't understand, Master," Obi-Wan said. "I know you're worried about Master Adi and the other Jedi. But what if we reach Rhinnal and everyone is fine, and it was merely an equipment malfunction that prevented us from contacting the Jedi chapter house?"

"If that's the case, we'll leave Rhinnal and pursue the Bartokk freighter immediately," Qui-Gon responded. "But if the Jedi need our help, we'll be there for them."

Ever since Qui-Gon had mentioned that Adi Gallia once saved his life, Obi-Wan suspected his Master's concern for Adi Gallia was highly personal. He even imagined it was possible that Qui-Gon felt he owed something like a life debt to the other Jedi Master. Although Obi-Wan did not share his Master's sentimentality, he was increasingly curious to hear Qui-Gon's account of the adventure with

Adi Gallia. Still, Obi-Wan was silent. He didn't want Qui-Gon to think he was *too* interested. He turned away and found himself looking out the cockpit's viewport.

Bama threw a lever. Outside the viewport, the stars appeared to elongate into brilliant white streaks and the *Metron Burner* zoomed forward at incredible speed. A moment later, the ship entered hyperspace with a thunderous roar. Obi-Wan rested his eyes as the Corellian freighter began its faster-than-light journey to Rhinnal.

And to whatever danger awaited.

CHAPTER TWO

After leaving Darth Sidious's lair, Darth Maul went directly to the dimly lit hangar where he kept his starship. Twenty-six-and-a-half meters long, the shovel-nosed, knife-edged ship had originated as a Star Courier manufactured by Sienar Design Systems. The entire vessel had been extensively customized in a secret laboratory to become the perfect vehicle for Maul's covert missions. It was called the Sith Infiltrator.

The Infiltrator had six low-profile laser cannons, sophisticated sensor and tracking systems, and a class 3.0 hyperdrive. For sublight travel, it was equipped with an experimental high-temperature ion engine system that required large, retractable radiator panels that folded in during landings. On the port side, a cargo drop panel contained Sith "dark eye" probe droids, numerous weapons, and Maul's speeder bike.

Then there was the cloaking device. While most scientists considered invisibility fields to be theoretical, the Sith had already developed a powerful cloak field generator for the Infiltrator. Contained within the ship's distinctive long prow, the generator enabled the entire vessel and its contents to vanish or rematerialize with the ease of a shadow.

Darth Maul walked to a ramp that extended from the rear of the Infiltrator to the hangar floor. At the bottom of the ramp stood a golden protocol droid, designated C-3PX.

The droid trained his red photoreceptors on Darth Maul. Although C-3PX resembled an ordinary Cybot Galactica TC protocol droid, his body contained eighty-three concealed weapons. Darth Maul knew the exact location and function of each weapon, for he himself had modified the droid to be the Infiltrator's sentry.

Since C-3PX had nothing to report, he remained silent. The Sith Lord despised unnecessary communication and had programmed the droid to speak only when absolutely necessary. Maul swept up the ramp and into the ship, followed by C-3PX's clanking footsteps.

Inside the Infiltrator's control room, C-3PX strapped himself into one of the passenger seats while Maul readied the ship for launch. As soon as the engines fired, Maul piloted the Infiltrator out of the hangar, then up and away from Coruscant.

Maul punched the coordinates for the Esseles system into the nav computer and let the Infiltrator's autopilot take over while he checked the power cell on his double-bladed lightsaber. It was fully charged. Maul had never battled Bartokks.

But that's what he would have to do, if they stood in his way.

As the *Metron Burner* soared through hyperspace, Leeper made an adjustment to the nav computer. "We'll be arriving at Rhinnal in less than a minute," the droid announced.

Bama Vook swiveled in his seat to face the two Jedi. "Have either of you been to Rhinnal before?"

"Obi-Wan hasn't, but I visited once," Qui-Gon admitted. "It was many years ago, during the expansion of the Jedi chapter house. Building materials had to be delivered because so much of the planet's surface was still covered by ice."

"You'll find Rhinnal hasn't changed much," Bama chuckled. "Terraforming has created new forests, but it's still colder than a mynock's wingtips."

The nav computer blinked in anticipation of the Rhinnal system. Bama reached forward with one furry fist and pushed back on a lever, causing the *Metron Burner* to shudder as it exited hyperspace. Outside the cockpit, stationary stars materialized against the dark backdrop of space.

Obi-Wan looked up through the top of the cockpit canopy to see Rhinnal. The icy planet was covered with snow-capped mountains, rolling tundras, and frigid rivers. It resembled a great white ball with gray and blue streaks across its surface.

Bama piloted his freighter through a tight rotation, reorienting the *Metron Burner*'s flight path so Rhinnal appeared below the freighter. "Send a signal to the Jedi chapter house, Leeper," Bama ordered. "Tell them we want clearance for landing."

Leeper entered a message into the ship's comm unit, pressed a green button to send the transmission to Rhinnal, then waited. After ten seconds without a response, the droid tried again.

"Why isn't anyone answering?" Bama asked.

"I suggest we fly down at once, Bama. I will direct you to the Jedi chapter house."

Following Qui-Gon's instructions, Bama steered the *Metron Burner* into a deep dive toward Rhinnal's southern hemisphere. The freighter descended rapidly through a thick layer of clouds, then sharply leveled off two kilometers above the planet's snow-covered surface.

A wide, slate-gray river snaked across the terrain, occasionally branching off into smaller rivulets that permeated the surface of the planet like crackled veins. On a wide tract to the north of the river lay a vast city of squat towers and domed structures. It was Rhire, the largest city on Rhinnal.

Although Rhinnal was originally a colony world of Esseles, there was little resemblance between Rhire and Calamar. Instead of roads, an extensive network of lift tubes and tunnels were used to travel throughout Rhire. The buildings were designed for the harshest weather conditions, and many utilized both solar and hydroelectric energy.

"The lights are off in all the buildings," Bama observed. "It seems there's a blackout all over the city."

Qui-Gon reached forward so his arm projected out over Leeper's shoulder. He aimed a finger in the direction of a low, semicircular building with two tall spires. "That's the Jedi chapter house," Qui-Gon said.

The building wrapped around a black, discoid landing pad. The landing pad had a ceramic coating on which snow and ice could not accumulate. Bordered by so much snow, it looked like an immense dot on the landscape. Nine hangars were built into the wall that surrounded the pad.

Bama brought the *Metron Burner* down near an open hangar door. The moment the *Metron Burner* settled down, Bama activated the control to lower the landing ramp. "Be sure to grab an anorak from the storage locker on the way out," he cautioned. "You don't need a thermometer to know it's more than a little chilly outside."

While Bama and Leeper switched off the freighter's systems, Qui-Gon and Obi-Wan unbuckled their safety belts and headed to the storage locker. Obi-Wan winced as he pulled a musty anorak over his head. "Doesn't this ship have a laundry unit?" he grumbled.

"You'll get a taste of fresh air soon enough," Qui-Gon replied.

A blast of icy wind hit Qui-Gon and Obi-Wan as they descended the freighter's ramp to the black landing pad. As they crossed the pad and entered the hangar, they sighted a hooded alien wearing a heavily padded parka. The alien appeared to be inspecting the Republic Cruiser *Radiant VII*, the same ship that had transported the Jedi from Coruscant to Esseles. At the alien's back, strips of shredded fabric dangled where two slits had been torn from the parka to accommodate a pair of broad, leathery wings. Hearing Qui-Gon and Obi-Wan enter, the winged figure turned and pulled off his fur-lined hood to reveal the tapered ears of a Baxthrax.

"Master Qui-Gon and Obi-Wan!" the Jedi Knight Noro Zak exclaimed. "I thought you'd still be in the Esseles system. Did you locate all the droid starfighters?"

"Only twenty-five," Qui-Gon answered. "We believe the remaining starfighters are en route to Corulag on a Bartokk freighter. We were able to transmit a warning of a possible attack to Corulag Academy, but I became concerned when we couldn't get a response from anyone here on Rhinnal."

Just then, Bama and Leeper stepped down from the *Metron Burner* and approached the hangar. After Qui-Gon introduced them to Noro, Bama asked, "So, what caused the blackout?"

"An electromagnetic storm shut down most of Rhire's power and all of Rhinnal's communications satellites," Noro explained. "The storm passed

CHAPTER THREE

The Sith Infiltrator's hyperspace journey from Coruscant to the Esseles system passed without incident. Maul had used the time to install the droid starfighter-controlling data card into the Infiltrator's main computer. As soon as Darth Maul entered the orbit of Esseles, he activated his ship's powerful scan-mode sensors.

The sensors sent out pulses in all directions, gathering information from the entire Darpa Sector. Maul adjusted the scanner, tuning it to search for and track any objects that moved in a trajectory away from Esseles. He narrowed the search further by transmitting a request for identification profiles from every outgoing starship within range.

Maul viewed a monitor that displayed the collected information: a list of fifty-eight starships, their respective sublight speeds, and their distances from Esseles. Maul did not expect any vessel to declare itself as a freighter filled with insectoid assassins and stolen Trade Federation property, so he was not surprised when only fifty-seven ships automatically responded with their ID profiles.

One ship had withheld its identification.

Maul checked the coordinates of the unknown ship. According to the Infiltrator's nav computer, the ship was still in the Darpa Sector, traveling through the Ralltiir system on a direct bearing for the planet Corulag. The Infiltrator's sensors could not determine whether the distant ship was the Bartokk freighter, but Maul would find out soon enough.

He plotted the course for the Ralltiir system and launched the Sith Infiltrator into hyperspace. After he made a final check to the nav computer, Maul swiveled his seat to face C-3PX. The droid remained seated on the other side of the small bridge. "What do you know about Ralltiir?" Maul asked.

C-3PX tilted his head slightly to the side before he replied. "It's a neutral world, and the only planet in the Darpa Sector that has maintained independence from the political control of Esseles. Ralltiir's financial institutions have an intergalactic reputation for their security and confidentiality."

Darth Maul nodded his head. "Are you familiar with Bartokk assassins?"

"They are an insectoid species with strong exoskeletons. There are fifteen Bartokks in every hive. They share a collective mind and communicate with each other by telepathy. Their intelligence is distributed throughout their nervous system, allowing any severed body part to perform independently from the body. This characteristic makes them difficult to kill."

On Maul's command console, a warning light flashed as the Infiltrator reached the Ralltiir system. Seconds later, the cruiser decelerated and reentered realspace. From the Infiltrator's bridge, the planet Ralltiir was clearly visible through Darth Maul's viewport. The mystery ship, on the other hand, was gone.

Maul consulted his sensor screens for the coordinates of the unidentified vessel's last noted location. From that point in space, an invisible trail of charged particles led off toward the planet Ralltiir. The Infiltrator's sensors confirmed that the particles had been left in the wake of the parting ship's sublight engines.

Darth Maul piloted the Infiltrator toward Ralltiir and entered the planet's orbit. "The Bartokks stole fifty Trade Federation droid starfighters and a prototype hyperdrive engine from a starship factory on Esseles," Maul notified the droid. "Sensors indicated the Bartokks were destined for Corulag. They changed course for Ralltiir, possibly because they intercepted my long-range scan and now hope to evade pursuit. My objective is to learn who hired the Bartokks, retrieve Trade Federation property, and terminate the Bartokks."

C-3PX's photoreceptors dimmed as he processed the data, then he asked, "Do you want to know the odds against completing your objectives?"

"Failure is not an option, so the odds are insignificant. I have informed you of the Bartokks because you may be required to run interference on Ralltiir."

The droid's photorececptors brightened. "It is unlikely that the Bartokks believe they can hide from us on Ralltiir. If they suspect they are being followed, there is a high probability they landed on the planet to prepare a trap."

"Naturally," Darth Maul replied. He used the sensors to get a fix on the charged particles that would lead him to the unidentified starship. Gripping the controls, the Sith Lord commandeered his Infiltrator into a rapid descent toward Ralltiir's surface. Without looking at the C-3PX, Maul stated, "I'll delay my attack until their guard is down."

C-3PX thought about this for a moment, then asked, "If the Bartokks are preparing a trap, when will their guard be down?"

Darth Maul glared at the droid. "After I let them catch me."

The trail of charged particles led to a mountainous region of Ralltiir, thirty-eight kilometers northwest of the city Grallia. Darkness had already fallen over the region, but the blanket of night hid little from the Sith Infiltrator's sensors. Darth Maul used the tracking sensors to follow the particle trail over a high, jagged rock formation.

Maul surmised that the elusive freighter's crew probably expected any attack to come from above.

Although he planned on surrendering to the crew, he had no intention of making it look easy. He activated the Infiltrator's cloaking device, and the ship vanished from sight as it flew over the jagged rocks.

While the cloaking device prevented the Infiltrator from being viewed by outsiders, the cruiser's interior was visible to Maul and C-3PX. Maul checked the sensors and saw that the particle trail ended at the rim of a wide canyon. High on the canyon's east wall, a great fortress was built into the side of the cliff.

Scanning the terrain, Maul found an opportunity for an indirect approach to the canyon. He piloted the cloaked Infiltrator low over a broad mesa, and then plunged into a deep ravine. Maintaining a high speed, he steered through the narrow gap between the stark mountain walls, then leveled off ten meters above the gorge.

The treacherous ravine led into the wide canyon. Maul flew behind a towering butte that rose from the base of the canyon, well out of visual range from the high cave. He prepared for landing and deactivated the cloaking device. The Infiltrator rematerialized, and its now-visible wings folded in as Maul brought the ship down beside the butte.

"The ship's particle trail indicates it flew directly to a remote fortress," Maul told C-3PX. "It might be a Bartokk hideout. I'll fly my speeder to the fortress and break in. You guard the Infiltrator."

C-3PX nodded, but Maul had already left the bridge.

Armed with only his lightsaber, Maul stepped out of the Infiltrator and drew his electrobinoculars from his belt. He held them up to his yellow eyes and adjusted the night vision control, then scanned the rim of the canyon until he located the fortress. It was at least seven stories high, as indicated by the positions of small inset windows. Three domed turrets loomed like guardian silos over a granite roof. Despite the architectural details, the structure blended so well with the surrounding natural stones that Maul imagined it had been carved out of the mountain itself.

Maul magnified his view of the inset windows. With the exception of one small, unlit window at the lowest level, all the others were barred. The unbarred window appeared to be the best access into the fortress.

After Maul returned the macrobinoculars to his belt, he deployed his saddle-shaped speeder from the underside cargo hatch. Unlike the Infiltrator, the speeder was not equipped with any sensors, weapons, or shields, but it was capable of astonishing velocity and maneuverability. On any planetary environment, it was Maul's preferred means of transportation.

He climbed onto his speeder and gunned the repulsorlift engine. The engine had been designed for maximum performance and minimum noise. Maul's victims rarely heard the speeder's approach until it was too late.

The speeder shot forward and raced across the dark canyon floor. Maul used the Force to sense each obstacle. He flew close to the base of the east wall, then pulled back into a vertical climb to the fortress above. Gripping the controls, the Sith Lord sank hard against his seat as the speeder rose, resisting Ralltiir's gravitational pull.

Maul landed the speeder on a rocky ledge just below the fortress's first level. In a fluid motion, he switched off the engine and dismounted the speeder. Maul ignored the cold, thin air as he quickly scaled the wall to the dark open window.

With predatory stealth, Maul slipped through the window and perched on the sill. The window was set nearly four meters above the floor of what appeared to be a cellar storage room. Except for a few empty food crates, the room was empty.

It was all too accessible. Maul knew the room was probably a trap, but he was looking forward to confronting the Bartokks. With that in mind, he jumped down from the window.

As soon as his feet hit the floor, the storage room was filled with an intensely bright light. Maul threw an arm up over his eyes to protect his vision, and heard the sound of a metal shield slamming into place from above. The high window had been automatically sealed.

Maul lowered his arm and squinted at two bright spotlights that were set within the inner walls. He heard a door slide open, followed by a digitized voice that cautioned, "One wrong move and you'll be fried. Raise your hands over your head."

Because of the light, Maul could not see the speaker, but he lifted his hands. A second later, he felt a tug at his waist as his lightsaber was snatched from his belt. At the same time, both of Maul's hands were grasped tightly and yanked down to the small of his back. He heard a snap as durasteel binders were clamped around his wrists, securing his arms behind him.

"Now step forward," the digitized voice commanded. "Slowly."

Maul passed through a doorway and entered a low-ceilinged corridor. His eyes were still recovering from the spotlights when he felt a sharp jab at his back.

"Keep moving," threatened the voice from behind. At the end of the corridor, a door slid back into the wall, and Maul was urged to step through the open passage.

Maul blinked as he entered an immense inner courtyard. Illuminated only by the star-filled sky above, the rectangular courtyard had been re-designed as a docking bay. At its center, sur-rounded by the three silo-like towers, rested a huge, spike-covered Bartokk freighter. Examining the vessel, Maul noticed a six-winged Bartokk starfighter secured to the freighter's outer hull.

"Halt," Darth Maul's captor ordered. Maul obeyed.

The freighter's main cargo door opened, and a retractable ramp extended from the ship to the ground. A procession of Trade Federation droid starfighters, with their wings configured in walk-ing patrol mode, marched down the freighter's ramp. They filed into the courtyard, and lined up in a square five-by-five formation. Even at rest, they were an intimidating sight.

Eleven Bartokks were stationed around the freighter. All were heavily armed with spears and bowcasters. The insectoids watched through bul-bous eyes as Darth Maul's captor stepped away from his prisoner. The captor was also a Bartokk, yet this particular assassin wore an expensive vo-cabulator on a chain around his lean neck.

"Why did you break into our fortress?" the Bar-tokk asked.

Darth Maul did not answer.

The Bartokk's mandibles clicked together. "Our sensors picked up a scan from Esseles. We believe you are the one who scanned our freighter. Instead of fighting in space, we decided to lure you here. You will tell us your name and affiliation."

Darth Maul remained silent.

The Bartokk held up Darth Maul's lightsaber. "This is the weapon of the Jedi. You are a Jedi Knight?"

The Sith Lord stared directly ahead and said nothing.

The Bartokk ignored Maul's lack of response and said, "Despite your ship's invisibility field, we tracked your landing. We know the vessel is at the base of the canyon, and sent a team to get it."

Maul's face did not betray any emotion, but he seethed at the Bartokk's words. The Infiltrator's cloaking device was engineered to evade any standard tracking sensor, but the Bartokks were fortunate to have sensors that were better than standard.

The Bartokk then craned his head back to look up at the night sky. Maul followed his gaze to see a small repulsorlift skiff soar over the fortress's west wall, then descend into the courtyard. At the helm of the skiff stood two Bartokks. Behind them, C-3PX was chained to the rear deck railing. Maul knew the droid could easily break free of the Bartokks' chains, and realized the droid had followed his own plan by allowing himself to be taken prisoner.

The skiff landed near Darth Maul and the vocabulator-equipped Bartokk. Like Maul, C-3PX's wrists were also secured behind his back by dura-steel binders. The droid began speaking in a worried tone as two Bartokks hoisted him off the skiff and onto the ground.

"These creatures arrived immediately after you left, sir," C-3PX said, his voice filled with worry and dread. "I managed to secure your ship and prevented them from boarding, but I'm afraid I couldn't do anything to prevent my capture."

"Quiet, droid," Maul muttered. In truth, Maul was pleased by C-3PX's acting ability. If Maul had not been responsible for programming the droid, he would have been convinced C-3PX was nothing more than nervous.

"A team will be sent to strip your ship for any vital information," the vocabulator-equipped Bartokk said as he slapped a restraining bolt on C-3PX's metal chest. "You will be taken to separate cells and interrogated."

Darth Maul and C-3PX were each escorted by a pair of Bartokks and led out of the courtyard. Maul had so far sighted fourteen Bartokks, but there were fifteen to a hive. Since droid starfighters were operated by remote control, Maul suspected the fifteenth Bartokk had stayed within the freighter to direct the starfighters.

The Sith Lord, the droid, and their four Bartokk

escorts descended a flight of stone steps and walked to a filthy dungeon, where ten cell doors lined a dim corridor. The corridor's floor was a series of metal grates, and C-3PX's feet clanked loudly with each step. Without breaking his pace, Maul glanced down through the open slits between the grates. He tried to determine what was below the corridor floor, but he saw only darkness.

The Bartokks opened two cell doors and gestured for Maul and the droid to step into separate cells. Remaining in the corridor, the four Bartokks slammed the doors shut.

Darth Maul's cell was illuminated by a single glow rod embedded over the door. A rusted metal bedframe was braced to a corner, and there was a puddle of greasy slime on the floor. The small chamber reeked of rot.

Now that he was tucked away in a cell, Maul believed the Bartokks would let down their guard. He decided it was time to begin his attack on the insectoid assassins. He was contemplating the best way to break out of the cell when he heard a whirring sound above his head. Maul instinctively took a step backward.

A black barrel-shaped interrogation droid hovered down from the ceiling. It came to a stop and hung in the air in front of Maul's face. Five retractable arms extended from the droid, and each servo-grip clasped a laser scalpel. The droid sputtered a burst of threatening static, then droned, "Before I terminate you, do you wish to make a statement?"

"Yes," Darth Maul hissed through clenched teeth. "This entire fortress is going to burn."

At this point, you must decide whether to continue reading this adventure, or to play your own adventure in the Star Wars Adventures *The Fury of Darth Maul* Game Book.

To play your own adventure, turn to the first page of the Game Book and follow the directions you find there.

To continue reading this Jedi adventure, turn the page!

CHAPTER FOUR

Within the confines of the wretched cell, the interrogator droid hovered a few centimeters away from Darth Maul, then trained its socketed photoreceptor on his face. The droid stared into Maul's yellow eyes, then snickered, "Think you're tough, huh? When I'm done with you, you won't be."

Behind his back, Maul flexed his wrists. The durasteel binders dug into his flesh, but the Sith Lord felt no pain. With a jerk, Maul pulled his arms apart. The binders shattered, scattering bits of durasteel all over the cell's filthy floor.

The interrogator droid made an excited whirring sound. It had never seen a prisoner break free from a set of binders with such ease. The droid activated its laser scalpels and hurtled through the air toward Maul.

Maul delivered a sharp kick to the droid's spherical underside. The droid soared toward the ceiling but regained control before impact and flew back toward the Sith.

Maul leaped aside, moving faster than the droid's photoreceptor could follow. The droid raced past him and smashed hard against the cell wall.

Although Maul's fight with the droid had caused plenty of noise, Bartokk guards did not burst into the cell. Maul assumed the cell walls were soundproofed or the Bartokks were confident he had just lost.

Smoke rose from the deactivated interrogator

droid. Maul stepped over its smoldering parts and examined the cell door. Locked from the outside, the door was heavily reinforced. But Maul was not concerned. He was about to break out when he noticed the remains of the interrogation droid on the floor. Its interrogation serum was intact.

Maul suspected the interrogation serum would be useful against a Bartokk. He unclamped the container from the droid's body and pocketed the device.

He returned his gaze to the cell door. Using the Force, he concentrated on the door's locking mechanism. He heard a clank as a heavy bolt slid back into the wall.

Darth Maul stepped out of the cell and onto the corridor's grated floor. Although four Bartokks had brought Maul and C-3PX into the dungeon, only two Bartokk escorts were posted outside the cells. The other cell doors remained sealed. The two Bartokks whirled to confront the escaped prisoner.

Maul leaped and landed beside the nearest Bartokk. Before the insectoid assassin could reach for a weapon, Maul snatched two poison-tipped arrows from the Bartokk's quiver. With one hand, Maul drove the arrow through the nearest Bartokk's armor-plated torso. With his other hand he flung an arrow at the second creature, catching it between its bulbous eyes. Both Bartokks fell to the grated floor.

Since the other cell doors remained sealed, it appeared C-3PX was still trapped. Darth Maul was about to free the droid when the other two Bartokk escorts appeared at the end of the corridor. Seeing Maul standing over their fallen comrades, one of the Bartokks struck a wall panel that controlled a series of trapdoors within the dungeon. Suddenly, the grated floor dropped away beneath Maul's feet. A second later, he plunged down through the trapdoor and into a dark cavern.

Maul landed on top of a sandpile and rolled to the subterranean floor. Lifting himself up, he looked at the cavern ceiling. The trapdoor had sealed, but Maul could see the Bartokks through the grated floor. The Bartokks scurried across the corridor and jammed twin-bolt crossbows down through the floor's open slots. They aimed their weapons at Maul and fired. Four poison-tipped, armor-piercing arrows sped toward the Sith Lord.

Maul's hands moved like lightning as he plucked each arrow from the air and flung them back at the assassins. The arrows shot up through the grated floor and struck the two snipers. Their arms reflexively reached to remove the arrows, but the poison worked rapidly.

Now there were four Bartokks lying on the corridor floor above Darth Maul. The trapdoor was sealed, and it was far too high for Maul to reach. He began to look for another way out of the cave.

A loud hiss stirred the air. Maul turned and saw a shadow shift against the rough rock walls. A reptilian head pushed forward from the dark, and a pair of large green eyes stared down at Maul from behind a wide reptilian mouth.

It was a draigon-slug. The gigantic snakelike creatures had been discovered living in caves on several worlds, but Maul was surprised to find one beneath the surface of Ralltiir. He suspected the Bartokks had imported the beast and kept it to discourage thieves from entering the caves. Draigon-slugs were fire-breathing monsters, and they had been known to devour their prey in a single bite.

Maul had no desire to slay the draigon-slug. Unlike the deliberately murderous Bartokks, the draigon-slug was simply a predator trying to protect its territory. To Maul's left, a tall stalagmite rose up from the cavern floor. It resembled an inverted, twisted cone. Maul dove behind the stalagmite and waited for the draigon-slug to pass.

But the draigon-slug didn't pass. It slithered around the stalagmite, found Maul's concealed position, and opened its maw. Maul knew he would have to defend himself. He ran toward the creature, jumped over its back, and wrapped his arms around the end of its tail. As the draigon-slug twisted to bite his attacker, Maul dragged the draigon-slug's tail toward its stomach and tricked the creature into forming a loop. Before the draigon-slug realized what was happening, Maul pulled the tail around its looped body. The creature was instantly tangled by its own elongated form.

Maul left the writhing draigon-slug to untie itself and advanced through the cave. He stepped around another stalagmite and discovered the entrance to a tunnel in the cavern wall.

The tunnel led to an underground chamber with a high, vaulted ceiling. On the far end of the chamber, Maul saw what appeared to be another tunnel. As he approached, the path ended at a ledge that rode the edge of a broad, deep chasm. From the ledge to the next tunnel, the distance across the chasm was at least nine meters. Although Maul was confident he could jump the nine-meter span, he did not know whether the ground was stable on the other side. He looked for an alternative route.

Dozens of long, securely moored stalactites dangled down from the chamber's ceiling. Darth Maul imagined he would be able to travel hand-over-hand from one stalactite to another until he reached the other side of the chasm. Maul was considering whether to jump the chasm or scale the ceiling when he noticed a mammoth spydr clinging to the cavern wall behind him.

The spydr had nine long, powerful legs. It appeared to be asleep, with its thick, hair-covered abdomen slowly rising and falling with each breath. Still, Maul kept his eyes on it as he clambered up the chamber wall to the stalactites.

Maul gripped a stalactite, then swung to grip another. The conical deposits were moist from dripping mineral water, and Maul was careful not to lose his grip on the slippery formations. He was halfway over the chasm when the giant spydr suddenly scurried up the wall and across the vaulted ceiling. It was not sleeping after all.

The spydr was not even tired.

CHAPTER FIVE

The spydr's mouth opened and closed, revealing many rows of sharp teeth. Darth Maul had no doubt the creature wanted him for dinner. He also knew if he let go of the stalactites he would fall into the chasm.

As the spydr crawled closer, Maul felt his fingers begin to lose their grip. When the spydr was within range, Maul swung both of his legs forward and kicked the creature in the head.

The injured spydr screeched and sprayed a thick web at Darth Maul. The Sith Lord released his right hand, grabbed the sprayed strand, and gave a sharp pull. The spydr did not sever its connection to the web in time and suddenly found itself being torn from the ceiling by Maul's tug. Maul let go of the strand and watched the spydr plummet into the chasm.

Undaunted, Darth Maul reached up, grabbed another stalactite, and resumed his crossing of the vaulted ceiling. Nine grips later, he completed the short journey and dropped down onto the ledge outside the next cave.

The cave led directly to a flight of smooth stone steps. They were coated with a thin layer of moist slime, the result of condensation from the cavern. As Maul carefully climbed the slick stones, he saw an open doorway at the top of the flight.

A burned-out glow rod extended from an iron bar over the doorway. From where Maul stood on the stairs, it looked like the doorway led to a chamber that was illuminated by a red light. Maul suspected the doorway might lead back into the fortress. He crouched down at the top of the slime-covered steps and peered into the chamber.

The room contained a circular pool built into the floor. The pool was approximately three meters in diameter, and it was filled with a hot, bubbling fluid. Steam rose from it and carried the scent of chemical waste.

Next to the pool, a thick-linked chain hung from a pulley secured to the ceiling. At the end of the chain, a hook was secured to a set of metal fetters that gripped a green-skinned female alien by her ankles. Hanging upside down over the pool, she was tied up with rope. She had the reptilian skin and facial structure of a Falleen. Her head dangled a mere meter above the bubbling pool, and her eyes were wide with terror.

Beside the pool, a standing Bartokk faced the helpless Falleen. Darth Maul recognized the Bartokk as the same one who had sent him and C-3PX to the dungeon. The Bartokk still wore the vocabulator around his neck, and his upper right arm wielded the confiscated lightsaber. The lightsaber's two shimmering blades filled the room with the flickering luminescence, and its hum reverberated in the air. The Bartokk did not appear to be carrying any other weapons, but Maul noticed a restraining bolt activator secured to his belt.

The Bartokk raised the lightsaber, bringing one of the blades dangerously close to the chain that kept the Falleen from falling into the bubbling pool. "The secrets of our mission will die with you," the Bartokk threatened his victim.

Darth Maul did not know how the Falleen was involved in the Bartokks' schemes, but if she knew any secrets, he wanted her to share them. He extended his right hand toward the Bartokk and concentrated on his plundered lightsaber.

Unable to resist the power of the Force, the Bartokk's claw opened and released the activated lightsaber. The weapon spun through the air like a lethal baton until it reached Darth Maul's grasp. His right hand lashed out and grabbed his lightsaber by its central grip.

The Bartokk turned to face Maul, then took a cautious step backward, closer to the bubbling pool. Suddenly, two more Bartokks dropped down from a hiding place above the doorway. They carried sharp spears.

The vocabulator-equipped Bartokk chittered, then said, "You forget that we Bartokks communicate telepathically. Before your four escorts perished in the dungeon, one of them alerted us of your escape. We knew if you survived the dangers

in the cavern, you would eventually enter here."
The Bartokk extended a claw toward the Falleen,
and added, "We produced this image to make certain we would lure you into this chamber."

As the Bartokk gestured with his claw, the Falleen wavered, faded, then vanished into thin air,
leaving the chain and hook dangling over the pool.
The tied-up alien had been a holographic projec-
tion. Nothing more than a trick.

Darth Maul hated to be tricked.

CHAPTER SIX

The three Bartokks in the subterranean chamber had earned Darth Maul's wrath. He fixed the two spear-wielding Bartokks with his piercing gaze, then pounced.

Maul's lightsaber tore through one Bartokk, severing his upper body at the waist and cutting his spear in half. In passing through the Bartokk, Maul's blade instantly cauterized the assassin's wounds, and only a drop of the Bartokk's black blood hit the floor. The Bartokk's upper body landed on its lower arms while the upper arms clung to the broken spear.

The second spear-wielding Bartokk hurled his weapon at Maul, but the Sith Lord easily dodged it. Before the spear clattered against the wall, the Bartokk extended all his claws and lunged. Maul brought his lightsaber up fast and gave it a neat spin, slicing the Bartokk's claws off with the first turn, and then lopping off his head with the second. Even though the Bartokk's skull was protected by his exoskeleton armor, his head hit the floor with an ugly noise.

The two Bartokks' dismembered limbs all scrambled and clawed for Darth Maul. To avoid the crawling carnage, he leaped up into the air and executed a backward somersault, then landed hard. Maul swung his lightsaber and kicked at the body parts, sending them into the toxic pool.

During Maul's battle with the two Bartokks, the

vocabulator-equipped Bartokk remained off to the side of the chamber, monitoring Maul's every move. Seeing his two comrades perish, the surviving Bartokk snatched a fallen spear from the floor.

Maul wanted to get information out of the Bartokk. He was determined to take him alive. Out of the corner of one eye, Maul noticed the metal hook swinging back and forth at the end of the chain that dangled from the ceiling. Below the hook, the toxic pool continued to bubble and steam.

As the Bartokk sprang, Darth Maul used the Force to propel the metal hook through the air. The hook snagged the Bartokk, catching him before the chain snagged at the pulley. The Bartokk swung out in a broad arc, struggling to free himself from the sharp hook as he dangled over the toxic pool.

Maul removed the restraining bolt activator from the Bartokk's belt, then stated, "You're going to answer some questions."

"You won't get a word out of me," the Bartokk replied in a gravelly voice.

Maul produced the container he had removed from the interrogation droid. It held a full dose of Bavo Six, a powerful truth serum. Without further hesitation, Maul jumped up on top of the winch, reached out, and introduced the serum into the Bartokk's system.

"I want to know the name of your client and why you stole the Trade Federation droid starfighters," Maul demanded as he deactivated his lightsaber.

Panic was visible in the Bartokk's bulbous eyes as the truth serum worked its way through his nervous system. Reluctantly, he answered, "We were hired by Groodo the Hutt. He owns a factory on Esseles that specializes in the manufacture of customized hyperdrive engines. Our job was to destroy Corulag Academy, but to make it look like the Trade Federation was responsible."

Darth Maul considered the Bartokk's response, and realized he now had more questions. "Why did Groodo want to blame the Trade Federation, and how did he know the droid starfighters were on Esseles?"

"The Trade Federation had secretly commissioned Groodo to construct a prototype hyperdrive engine, but they refused to pay him," the Bartokk replied. "Groodo placed a sensor tag on the prototype. He tracked the sensor tag to Trinkatta Starships, where he discovered Trinkatta was constructing fifty droid starfighters. The Hutt hired us to steal the prototype engine as well as the starfighters."

"I saw only twenty-five droid starfighters in the landing bay," Maul commented. "Where are the other twenty-five droid starfighters and the prototype hyperdrive engine now?"

"They were in another freighter," the Bartokk answered. "It was overtaken by the Jedi."

The Jedi. Darth Maul was not surprised they were involved. Now he could think of only two more questions. "Why does Groodo want to destroy Corulag Academy, and where is he now?"

The Bartokk tried to fight the truth serum, but answered, "Groodo was angered that his son was denied admission to the Academy. Both Groodo and his son are now on their private cruiser, in orbit around Corulag. Groodo wants to watch the destruction of the Academy."

Darth Maul had to admit that Groodo's plan was cunning. By using the droid starfighters to blame the Trade Federation for an attack on Corulag Academy, the Hutt would have his revenge on both the unscrupulous Trade Federation and the discriminating Academy.

Without warning, one of the Bartokk's legs kicked at Darth Maul, knocking the Sith from the winch to the edge of the pool. Then, the Bartokk reached for a concealed weapon. It was a razoredged boomerang. The Bartokk drew his arm back and threw the boomerang at Maul.

The Sith Lord activated his lightsaber and swung at the oncoming boomerang. The lightsaber's blade barely glanced Bartokk's weapon, but the contact was enough to launch the boomerang straight for the metal chain that hung above the pool. The boomerang cut clean through the chain, and the Bartokk plunged down into the toxic pool with a great splash. Maul watched as the Bartokk's body rapidly melted.

Maul deactivated his lightsaber and proceeded to the far end of the chamber. There he found a narrow doorway that led to a circular staircase. Cautiously, he moved up the stairs, which wrapped around a central stone column, until he reached a large room on the first-floor level of the fortress. The room was piled high with explosives and assorted munitions.

A plastic box filled with thermal detonators caught Darth Maul's attention. The detonators were shaped like small metal balls and resembled standard grenades, but they contained a powerful synthetic explosive called baradium.

Maul immediately contemplated setting the timer on a single detonator and leaving it in the volatile munitions room. The destruction of so many baradium-filled weapons would cause an explosion that might bring down the entire fortress. Since the detonator's timer offered a maximum countdown of ten minutes, Maul knew he would have to leave the fortress fast.

There was only one setback. For all Maul knew, it was possible that C-3PX was still trapped within the fortress' dungeon. If the droid had not already escaped, there would be little chance for his survival.

Maul set the timer on a thermal detonator for a ten-minute countdown. As he placed the detonator back in the plastic box, he removed a second detonator and clipped it to his belt. Maul liked to be prepared.

He left the munitions room and quickly found his way through the fortress until he reached the courtyard. There, under the light of Ralltiir's moons, the spike-covered Bartokk freighter remained on the landing pad. To Maul's surprise, the freighter's main cargo door was still wide open.

Just beyond the freighter, he saw two Bartokks standing beside their repulsorlift skiff. They had retrieved his speeder, and were unloading it from the skiff. The Sith Lord considered making a break for the speeder, but he needed to find out what had happened to the twenty-five droid starfighters.

He walked around the freighter and found that the droid starfighters were gone, along with the six-winged Bartokk starfighter that had been docked to the freighter. Since the Trade Federation droid starfighters were controlled by a central droid computer, it seemed likely that the Bartokk starfighter was carrying the control computer and guiding the fighters to Corulag. The six-winged starfighter would have needed a crew of three Bartokks, which left at least five Bartokks on Ralltiir.

Unlike the Bartokk freighter, the departed starfighters had been engineered for hyperspeed. To pursue the droid starfighters to Corulag, Darth Maul knew he would have to return to the Sith Infiltrator.

But first he wanted to board the freighter and take the Bartokks' tracking sensor technology. Maul hoped the secured technology would enable him to prevent the Bartokks from tracking the Sith Infiltrator in cloak mode.

Maul consulted his chronometer. He had less than six minutes before the thermal detonator was timed to explode in the fortress. He had already decided that obtaining the Bartokks' tracking sensor data was worth the risk.

Over by the skiff, the two Bartokks were examining Maul's speeder. While they were preoccupied, Maul slipped up the freighter's landing ramp and entered the main cargo hold.

He ran through a murky corridor until he located the freighter's bridge. Like everything else on the freighter, the main computer console was designed to be operated by Bartokk claws. However, Maul was skilled at retrieving information from alien technology. He inspected the scanners and his fingers darted over the controls.

Seconds later, Maul found the sensor data. The Bartokks had used a highly sensitive sensor called a crystal gravitational trap to detect gravitational fluctuations generated by his cloaked ship. With this sensor, his cloaked ship could not hide from the Bartokks. Maul punched up a data card and downloaded the information. Maul believed the Sith Infiltrator's computers could examine the data and find a way for his cloaking device to elude the Bartokks' scans.

Maul turned away from the computer console and found himself facing another Bartokk. In each of his four claws, the Bartokk gripped a vibro-ax. The Sith Lord was amazed the assassin had been able to sneak up behind him, but his amazement immediately turned into defensive action.

The Bartokk whipped two of the vibro-axes at Maul. The Sith Lord darted to the side as he activated his lightsaber. The thrown vibro-axes sailed past him and slammed into the freighter's nav computer console, causing a small explosion.

The Bartokk charged, and Maul's lightsaber was a blur of bright crimson as he went for the assassin's wrists. In a single sweep of the lightsaber's blade, the Bartokk had lost all four of his claws. Two of the claws, still gripping vibro-axes, thrashed across the floor of the bridge.

The Bartokk leaped at Maul. Maul brought his foot up fast and caught the Bartokk hard. The Bartokk fell backward and landed on top of the vibro-axes clasped in his own claws. Seconds later, the Bartokk's severed parts were motionless.

Maul deactivated his lightsaber and returned it to his belt. Running down the murky corridor to the freighter's main cargo hold, he checked his chronometer. He had less than a minute to escape the fortress compound before the thermal detonator exploded.

He raced down the freighter's landing ramp and headed straight for his speeder bike. The two Bartokks were still so busy examining Maul's vehicle that they didn't see him running toward them. They stumbled back in surprise as he leaped onto his speeder.

Before the Bartokks could recover, Maul gunned the repulsorlift engine and shot out of the fortress's landing bay.

As Maul zoomed away from the fortress, he checked his chronometer again. In his head, he counted off the final seconds.

Five . . . four . . . three . . . two . . .

Behind him, the entire fortress was wracked by a massive, thunderous explosion. Maul looked over his shoulder to see the fortress lit up like daylight by the incredible blast. Raging fires swept up the three silo-like towers, then one of the towers buckled and fell, smashing down on the Bartokk freighter. Although Maul was a bit worried about the fate of C-3PX, he found the sound of the freighter's rupturing hull to be most satisfying.

Suddenly, a blaster bolt struck the side of Maul's speeder. Maul turned his head to cast a glance over his other shoulder and saw he was being pursued across the sky by the two Bartokks on their repulsorlift skiff.

As impossible as it was to conceive, they had escaped the explosion.

CHAPTER SEVEN

Flying the skiff across the night sky behind Darth Maul, both Bartokks gripped a set of navigational controls with their lower arms while their upper arms carried bowcasters. The blaster bolt that had struck Maul's speeder had been fired by one of the assassins. The two Bartokks were preparing to fire another volley at the swift speeder when Maul steered through a tight spin and angled back on a collision course for the skiff.

The Bartokks veered away from the oncoming speeder, and looped the skiff through the air in pursuit of Maul. The Sith's speeder plunged over the upper rim of the canyon and raced down to the canyon floor. Blaster bolts whizzed past his head from behind as the Bartokks tried to get a bead on him.

Maul calculated his velocity and the distance between his speeder and the Bartokks' skiff. He accelerated and steered his vehicle closer to the canyon wall. Then he reached for the thermal detonator on his belt, thumbed the detonator's activator switch, and released the metal ball into the air.

The detonator met the front end of the Bartokks' skiff. There was a loud explosion, and Maul felt a wave of intense heat at his back. He pulled up on his speeder's controls and blasted away from the canyon wall before any burning debris could touch him. The detonator had not only destroyed the Bartokks and their skiff, but had punched a deep impression into the canyon wall, forming a small crater.

Maul flew his speeder down to the canyon floor. The Sith Infiltrator was parked exactly where he had left it. As he angled his speeder toward the Infiltrator, he sighted a lone Bartokk guard standing on the ground near the stern of the starship. From the guard's relaxed stance, Maul determined he hadn't seen the approaching speeder.

While Maul's left hand gripped the speeder controls, his right hand reached for his lightsaber and activated its blade. As Maul neared the Infiltrator, the guard caught sight of him. Maul leaned hard to the side so that his speeder was practically sideways, then swung his crimson lightsaber. With dazzling speed, the Bartokk dodged the deadly blade and snagged the back of the speeder with his claws. Clinging to the powerful speeder, the Bartokk was yanked from the ground.

The Bartokk's weight brought the speeder's tail down, and the vehicle was thrown off balance by the unwelcome passenger. The Bartokk was about to attack with his claws when Maul gunned the engine and launched into a steep vertical climb. Maul didn't want to risk damaging his own speeder with his lightsaber, so he quickly deactivated the weapon and returned it to his belt. With his free hand, he reached back over his head and grabbed one of the Bartokk's wrists.

Maul braked and swung his arm with all his might. The Bartokk was flung from the speeder and into the air. Maul's free hand returned to the speeder's controls and he blasted away from the free-falling Bartokk.

Now that the Bartokk was out of the picture, Darth Maul landed his speeder next to the Infiltrator. At first, it seemed the Bartokk guard had left the ship untouched. But after Maul returned his speeder to its storage compartment in the Infiltrator's underside cargo hatch, he noticed deep scratches on the aft hatchway. Still, the hatch was sealed, so he assumed the Bartokks had not been able to breach his ship's security system. He opened the aft hatch, entered the Infiltrator, and headed to the bridge.

Maul knew if the Bartokk starfighter and twenty-five droid starfighters were traveling through hyperspace by way of the Perlemian Trade Route, they were probably already halfway to Corulag. The Infiltrator was equipped with a Sienar SSDS 11-A hyperdrive, which was more powerful than any of the Bartokk or Trade Federation droid starfighters. Even though the Bartokks had a head start, Maul believed he might actually beat them to the Corulag system.

After Maul initiated the launching sequence, the Infiltrator lifted off from the canyon floor and blasted into the sky. Barely a minute later, the Infiltrator left Ralltiir's stratosphere and entered space. Maul plotted a course for Corulag and was preparing to make the jump to hyperspace when a warning light flashed. The Infiltrator's computer had detected a malfunction with the hyperdrive motivator. Maul wondered if the Bartokks had tampered with his ship after all, so he ran a complete diagnostic. Fortunately, the Infiltrator's automated repair system was quickly able to repair the malfunction.

Maul entered the coordinates for Corulag into the nav computer and activated the hyperdrive. Outside the Infiltrator, the stars appeared to elongate away from the central point of his destination. In the next instant, the distorted starfield was filled with an intense light, and the Infiltrator raced into hyperspace.

Maul consulted a computer monitor to confirm the hyperdrive motivator was fully operational. But on the surface of the monitor's screen, Maul saw something he had not anticipated — a reflection of something moving behind him.

It was a Bartokk.

CHAPTER EIGHT

Maul spun in his seat to face the Bartokk. The assassin had managed to infiltrate the Infiltrator, and was already on board when Maul blasted off Ralltiir. The Bartokk stowaway stood in front of the aft hatch, clicking his mandibles together as he made a horrid chittering sound. He bent his lean-muscled legs and prepared to spring out at Maul.

Maul grabbed hold of his seat with one hand and reached for the control console with the other. He punched a switch and the aft hatch snapped open, causing all the air to race out of the bridge. While Maul clung to his seat, the Bartokk was sucked toward the open hatch.

The Bartokk extended his arms and legs and braced himself in the hatchway. As the air tore at his insectoid body, the assassin located a manual emergency switch within the hatch frame and struck it with his lower left arm's elbow. The hatch slammed shut with a violent clang, clipping off one of the Bartokk's toes.

As air was pumped to repressurize the Infiltrator, Darth Maul leaped from the command console. The last thing he wanted was a fight that might ruin the interior of his starship. He dove across the bridge and activated his lightsaber. The Bartokk raised a blaster and squeezed off three quick shots. Still in mid-leap, Maul swung at the blaster bolts and struck them away. The three bolts slammed back at the unprepared Bartokk. Before the assassin could fire again, Darth Maul was on top of him, slashing his lightsaber with expert precision.

Still speeding through hyperspace, the Infiltrator entered the Corulag system. The nav computer automatically deactivated the hyperdrive, and there was a slight shudder as the vessel reentered realspace.

Maul conducted a quick sensor scan of the Corulag system. There was no sign of the Bartokk or droid starfighters. As Maul had expected, his more powerful hyperdrive had managed to beat the enemy ships to Corulag.

Through a viewport, Maul saw the planet ten thousand kilometers away. Even though Corulag was located on the lucrative Perlemian Trade Route, it did not look like a remarkable world. However, it was home to several billion citizens and the prestigious Corulag Academy. At the Academy, students were trained to become members of the Exploration, Military, and Merchant Services for the Republic.

According to the vocabulator-equipped Bartokk, Groodo the Hutt had hired the assassins to destroy Corulag Academy after his son had been denied admission to the institution. The Bartokk also had said that Groodo intended to watch the Academy's destruction from his cruiser.

Maul activated his sensors and scanned the Corulag system for any orbiting vessels besides unmanned satellites. Only one blip appeared on his sensor screen.

As Maul traveled toward the orbiting vessel's location, the Infiltrator's telescopic sensors produced a magnified visual of a medium-sized cruiser. It was decked out with broad fins and large oval viewports, and the hull was painted in vibrant oranges and yellows. In Maul's estimation, such an ugly ship could only be owned by a Hutt.

Suddenly, the Infiltrator's hyperwave warning light began to pulsate. Twenty-six starfighters were about to exit hyperspace in Maul's proximity.

Maul activated the Infiltrator's cloaking device, and the invisibility shields came on-line. Just as his starship vanished, twenty-five droid starfighters and a single Bartokk starfighter entered realspace. The fighters zipped in fast, then their sublight engines took over and they decelerated to a relatively slow crawl. The droid starfighters were all in flight mode, with their wings retracted to maintain a sleek profile. Flying behind them, the six-winged Bartokk starfighter controlled each of their flight paths. Since the Bartokks took up most of the available space within their starfighter, Maul assumed they had a compact droid central control computer on board.

Darth Sidious's orders had been clear: Maul

could not allow the Bartokks to use the Trade Federation droid starfighters to assault Corulag Academy. If the Trade Federation were to be blamed for an attack on Corulag, it would draw unwanted attention to the Trade Federation in that sector, and possibly affect Darth Sidious' plans for the future.

Maul was contemplating the best way to defeat the starfighter armada when the Bartokks' ship approached his position. Since the Infiltrator was in cloak mode, Maul pulled back so the Bartokks would not collide with his starship. Their starfighter passed so close to the invisible Infiltrator that Maul could look through their fighter's triangular viewports and see the Bartokk pilot, gunner, and tailgunner seated back-to-back-to-back within.

Suddenly, the Bartokks were illuminated by a bright, flashing warning light in the cockpit, and all three assassins turned their insectoid heads to peer out the viewports in Maul's direction. Maul had been so confident in the Infiltrator's cloaking device, he had forgotten about the Bartokks' sophisticated sensors.

Now they knew where he was.

CHAPTER NINE

Before Maul could react, the Bartokk star-fighter swung away from the Infiltrator and all twenty-five droid starfighters turned toward his cloaked ship. Despite the Infiltrator's invisibility, all the starfighters had locked onto his position. The droid starfighters' wings snapped into attack mode, revealing their lethal blaster cannons.

Maul quickly took the data card he'd retrieved from the Bartokk freighter and inserted it into a computer port. The Infiltrator's computer analyzed the Bartokk's sensor information, and immediately transmitted a jamming signal to knock out the Bartokk starfighter's crystal gravitational trap sensor. Before the droid starfighters could fire a single shot, the Infiltrator had vanished from the Bartokk starfighter's sensors.

The droid starfighters began swerving through space on an erratic course. They appeared to be out of control, but Maul knew better. The Bartokks were piloting the droid starfighters by remote control, steering them on a weaving course in an effort to locate Maul's ship by way of a direct collision.

Maul accessed the data that had been supplied by Darth Sidious. With the flick of a switch, Maul seized control of the droid starfighters.

The Sith Lord targeted the Bartokk starfighter, and all twenty-five droid starfighters rotated in space and aimed their cannons at the six-winged fighter craft. Maul imagined the three Bartokks were more than startled. By Bartokk standards, it was possible they were even scared.

In a desperate effort to evade certain death, the Bartokk starfighter turned and sped away from Corulag. The Bartokk tailgunner fired a steady stream of energy bolts in the starfighter's wake, aiming at nothing he could see, but hoping he would hit his invisible enemy.

Leaving the droid starfighters behind, the cloaked Infiltrator pursued the Bartokks' fleeing ship. Maul poured on the speed, dodging the Bartokk tailgunner's random assault. The Infiltrator was armed with six low-profile laser cannons, and Maul directed all of them to fire at the Bartokks' ship.

The first two blasts punched a hole in the Bartokk starfighter's deflector shields. Blasts three and four hammered through their particle shields. The last two shots connected directly with the starfighter's hull. With their shields down, the Bartokks didn't have a chance. As their starfighter erupted in a great fireball, Darth Maul angled the Infiltrator back toward Corulag.

During Maul's battle with the Bartokks, the red-and-yellow cruiser had remained in orbit around Corulag. Although Maul still wasn't certain the cruiser belonged to Groodo the Hutt, he decided it was time to find out. With the Infiltrator still in full cloak mode, Maul flew toward the orbital cruiser. When he had drawn within firing range, he transmitted an emergency hail to the brightly painted vessel.

"Come in, Groodo," Maul uttered into his ship-to-ship comm unit.

Seconds later, the three-dimensional image of a corpulent Hutt appeared. Although the image was a bit fuzzy, the Hutt's lower lip was moving from side to side, and his thick cheeks looked like they were quite stuffed. Maul realized he had caught the Hutt during a meal.

"What's the meaning of this interruption?" the Hutt snarled.

"There won't be any attack on Corulag Academy," Maul stated.

"What?!" the Hutt sputtered. "I mean . . . I don't know what you're talking about!"

"You made a grave error when you ordered the Bartokks to steal from the Trade Federation," Maul responded. "Consider this fair warning: You have thirty seconds to evacuate your cruiser before I destroy it."

"You dare threaten the mighty Groodo?" the Hutt retorted. "Show yourself!"

"Twenty seconds," Maul replied.

"Who *are* you?" the Hutt demanded. There was not a trace of fear in his response, and he sounded only slightly annoyed.

Maul switched off the comm unit and signaled the droid starfighters to come in. He commanded them to target the cruiser. At the final second, he commanded them to open fire.

Although the Hutt's cruiser had a powerful deflector shield, it had not been engineered to endure the combined firepower of twenty-five starfighters at close range. From the Infiltrator, Darth Maul watched as the Hutt's entire cruiser was instantly enveloped in a massive burst of ion-fueled flame.

A single emergency life pod managed to blast away from the cruiser's wreckage. Maul focused the Infiltrator's sensors on the pod, and learned that it carried two life-forms. It appeared both Groodo the Hutt and his son had survived the destruction of their cruiser. Since Darth Sidious had specified that the Bartokks' client should live in fear, Maul allowed the pod to tumble toward Corulag.

The twenty-five droid starfighters hung like deadly ornaments in space. Although the Jedi had destroyed the other twenty-five, Darth Maul believed his Master, Darth Sidious, would be pleased that half the starfighters had been recovered.

Maul considered escorting the starfighters back to Trade Federation space, but he was disturbed by a single detail: C-3PX. It was highly unlikely that the droid had survived the devastating explosion on Ralltiir, but Maul didn't like the no-tion of C-3PX's body being discovered by any enemies. The Sith Lord decided to return to the distant fortress and search the ruins.

Maul programmed the droid starfighters to fly to a Neimoidian base in Trade Federation territory. Responding to his command, all twenty-five droid starfighters angled in the same direction, then fired their engines and zoomed off into hyperspace.

After the starfighters had left the Corulag system, Maul plotted a course for Ralltiir. Then he punched the controls for the hyperdrive, and the Infiltrator blasted into hyperspace.

As he traveled back to Ralltiir, Maul's thoughts turned to Groodo the Hutt. Darth Sidious had been confident that the Bartokks' client would somehow be useful if he were to live in fear of the Trade Federation, but Maul wondered . . . *Are Hutts really afraid of anything?*

CHAPTER TEN

At this point, readers who chose to follow the adventure in the Star Wars Adventure Game Book can return to *The Fury of Darth Maul*.

The emergency escape pod landed in a dense forest thirty-four kilometers southwest of Curamelle, the capital city of Corulag, and home of Corulag Academy. The pod had crashed down through heavy foliage before setting down between three tall, wide-trunked trees. The pod's hatch slid open and Groodo the Hutt slithered out onto the grass-covered ground, followed by his son. The younger Hutt was considerably smaller than his father, but he was of healthy size for his age.

Groodo carried a comlink that accessed a HoloNet transceiver in the escape pod. As he punched in a series of numbers to place an intergalactic call, he turned to his son and said, "Don't worry, Boonda. Your old man's going to make everything all right."

"Sure, Pop," said Boonda with a shrug. "Whatever you say."

On Ralltiir, at the site of what had only recently been the Bartokks' fortress, Darth Maul used the Force to lift a heavy boulder from a pile of rubble. Maul had used the Sith Infiltrator's sensors to scan the fortress ruins for any sign of C-3PX. The sensors penetrated deep below the collapsed floors and fallen walls, searching for any trace of metal that might belong to the golden assassin droid. Now, Maul found himself sifting through the area of what had been a chamber near the fortress's dungeon.

Maul did not watch the boulder as it levitated away through the air, and he ignored the loud thud, eight meters away, that sounded as he released the boulder from his power. The Sith Lord's yellow eyes were fixed on something that rested on the crushed floor, staring at something that had been concealed by the transplanted boulder.

It was a restraining bolt. The same bolt that had been placed on C-3PX by the vocabulator-equipped Bartokk.

The droid had escaped from his cell after all.

Darth Maul raised his gaze and surveyed the debris. All around him, thick black smoke rose from the fires that burned beneath the scattered debris. Except for the rising smoke, nothing else moved.

He looked at the Sith Infiltrator, resting on a flat level of earth at a safe distance from the smoldering stones. Although Maul trusted his starship's sensors, he relied even more on his own senses. He closed his eyes and held his breath. He blocked out the sound of the small, crackling fires, and of the whispering wind that blew over the ruins, sending fine sand drifting down into the canyon. He tuned out all natural noise, and he listened for the faint hum of logic processors, the dull whir of a pelvic servometer, and the shuffling scuff of metal feet on rocky ground. But in the end, there was only the wind.

C-3PX was gone.

Darth Maul knew Darth Sidious would be expecting a full report back on Coruscant. Maul drew his dark cloak over his head, then walked swiftly to the Infiltrator.

He left no footprints.

At the Jedi chapter house on the ice planet Rhinnal, Obi-Wan Kenobi walked past a group of doctors and entered Adi Gallia's spacious, brightly lit medical suite. He found Qui-Gon Jinn standing at the foot of Adi Gallia's bed.

"Welcome, Obi-Wan," Adi Gallia said. She was seated on the edge of her mattress pad, and her dangling sandaled feet nearly touched the spotless white floor. The suite was designed to accommodate dignitaries, as was indicated by an expensive holocom console and tall picture windows.

Obi-Wan bowed his head. "I'm pleased to see you well, Master Adi." Despite the fact that Obi-Wan could barely contain his curiosity, he refrained from asking Adi Gallia to confirm that she had once saved Qui-Gon's life.

"The medics say she's almost fully recovered,"

Qui-Gon informed his apprentice. "We also noticed the lights have come back on. Has the magnetic storm passed?"

"Yes," replied Obi-Wan. "That's what I came to tell you. We're cleared to leave Rhinnal, and both the *Radiant VII* and *Metron Burner* are ready for launch."

"Were you able to get a message through to Corulag?" Qui-Gon asked.

Obi-Wan nodded. "A Corulag Space Traffic Control satellite reported an orbital space battle that took place less than an hour ago. Twenty-seven ships were involved in the skirmish: a Bartokk starfighter and an unidentified cruiser were destroyed. The other ships all sounded like Trade Federation droid starfighters, but they escaped into hyperspace."

"Could the cruiser have been the Bartokks' target?" Adi Gallia asked.

"It's unlikely," Qui-Gon replied, stroking his chin as he thought. "Bartokks are professional killers, not suicide squads. The Bartokk starfighter's purpose would have been to control the twenty-five droid fighters. If the cruiser had been the target, the Bartokks would have simply programmed the droid fighters to destroy it."

"Maybe the Bartokks were ambushed by the cruiser," Obi-Wan suggested.

"Perhaps," Qui-Gon allowed. "But we are still

left with an awkward question: Who has the droid starfighters now?"

Before anyone could offer an answer, a doctor entered the room. "Excuse me," she said, "but there's a HoloNet message holding for Qui-Gon Jinn. It's from Coruscant."

The doctor left Adi Gallia's suite, and Qui-Gon went to the holocomm console. He passed his hand over an ID scanner, then watched as a greenish light emanated from the holoprojector. The light flickered, then took on the unmistakable form of an old alien with wise eyes and long, sharply pointed ears.

"Master Yoda?" Qui-Gon said, genuinely surprised. "We were just about to leave for Corulag."

"Then late you *already* are," Yoda's hologram replied. "Meet you on Corulag, I will. Matters most urgent await us at the Academy. Go now at once!"

NEXT ADVENTURE:
JEDI EMERGENCY